Bumble and Bee

Let's BEE Thankful

ROSS BURACH

ACORN
SCHOLASTIC INC.

To Dave, Greta, and Miriam — RB

Library of Congress Cataloging-in-Publication Data
Names: Burach, Ross, author, illustrator.
Title: Let's bee thankful / Ross Burach.
Description: First edition. | New York : Acorn/Scholastic Inc., 2020. |
Series: Bumble and Bee ; 3 | Audience: Ages 4-6. | Audience: Grades K-1.
Summary: It is autumn, and Bumble and Bee are excited to paint pumpkins and help Froggy make a special
apple pie (if they can remember to fetch the butter); but when the weather turns colder it is time for Froggy to
settle into a cozy winter home—if only Bumble and Bee will leave Froggy alone.
Identifiers: LCCN 2020004544 (print) | LCCN 2020004545 (ebook) | ISBN 9781338505887 (v. 3 ; paperback) |
ISBN 9781338505894 (v. 3 ; hardback) | ISBN 9781338506204 (v. 3 ; ebk)
Subjects: LCSH: Bumblebees–Juvenile fiction. | Bees–Juvenile fiction. | Frogs–Juvenile fiction. |
Best friends–Juvenile fiction. | Autumn–Juvenile fiction. | Humorous stories. | CYAC: Bumblebees–Fiction. | Bees–
Fiction. | Frogs–Fiction. | Autumn–Fiction. | Best friends–Fiction. | Friendship–Fiction. | Humorous stories. | LCGFT:
Humorous fiction.
Classification: LCC PZ7.1.B868 Lc 2020 (print) | LCC PZ7.1.B868 (ebook) | DDC (E)–dc23

10 9 8 7 6 5 4 3 2 1   20 21 22 23 24
Printed in China   62
First edition, April 2020
Book design by Marijka Kostiw
Edited by Tracy Mack and Benjamin Gartenberg

Let's Paint
Pumpkins!

WE WISH FOR A PUMPKIN!

WE WISH FOR A PUMPKIN!!

WE WISH FOR A PUMPKIN!!!

It did not work.

Maybe Froggy can help us?

Froggy!

13

Well, we will **not** forget to get the butter!

Maybe I should write down **butter?**

Or we can just keep saying it!

Even better!

21

I do not see any **butter**.

Oh no!
We forgot!

This time we will not forget!

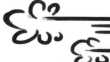

BUZZ-ZOOM!

Winter is almost here. I can feel it in the air.

It is my **favorite** season.

With just enough room for me, my blanket, my books, and my . . .

BEST FRIENDS!!!

Huh?

Wuh?

So we brought things to do!

The **BIG SQUISHY** ones?

Those are my favorite!

About the Author

Ross Burach lives with his family in Brooklyn, New York, where he spends his days drawing bees and frogs, and sharing hot cocoa and marshmallows with his family. He is the creator of the very funny picture books **The Very Impatient Caterpillar** and **Truck Full of Ducks**, as well as the board books **I Love My Tutu Too!**, **Potty All-Star**, and **Hi-Five Animals!**, named the best board book of the year by **Parents** magazine. Bumble and Bee is Ross's first early reader series.

YOU CAN DRAW BEE!

Bee creative!

1 To make Bee's body, draw most of a circle but don't close it. Add a small oval coming from the bottom of the circle. It should look like a lightbulb!

2 To make the eyes, draw two circles and two small dots inside. To make the mouth, draw a closed semicircle. Add a curved line for the tongue, and color in the rest.

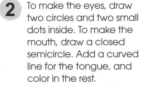

3 To make the antennae, draw two lines with tiny ovals at the ends. To make the wings, draw two upside-down U's with # signs inside.

4 To make the arms, draw two sets of parallel lines. To make the fingers, draw four joined U's at the end of each arm.

5 To make the nose, draw a line ending in a circle. Draw two thick stripes across Bee's body. Add a thick line for the stinger and four straight lines for legs.

6 Color in your drawing!

Nice work.

WHAT'S YOUR STORY?

Bumble and Bee are painting pumpkins!
What would **you** paint on a pumpkin?
Which colors would you use?
What can you add for decoration?
Write and draw your story!

scholastic.com/acorn